FOR SARAH AND SARAH

x x

Copyright © 2018 Morag Hood

Sourcebooks and the colophon are registered trademarks of Sourcebooks, Inc.

Lino print and collage were used to prepare the full color art.

Published by Sourcebooks Jabberwocky, an imprint of Sourcebooks, Inc.
P.O. Box 4410, Naperville, Illinois 60567-4410
(630) 961-3900
Fax: (630) 961-2168
sourcebooks.com

Originally published in 2018 in the United Kingdom by Two Hoots,
an imprint of Macmillan Publishers Ltd.

Library of Congress Cataloging-in-Publication Data is on file with the publisher.

Source of Production: LEO-Leo Paper-China, Heshan, Guangdong, China
Date of Production: May 2018
Run Number: 5012217

Printed and bound in China.
10 9 8 7 6 5 4 3 2 1

THE STEVES

MORAG HOOD

sourcebooks
jabberwocky

Hello! I'm Steve.

I'M Steve.

I am Steve.
You can be
Steve the
Second.

I am Steve
the First,

AH HA! I'm older than you. I am Steve! I am the greatest.

How many fish can you catch?

More than you.
I am the Champion
of Steves.
The Stevest
Steve.

I am the fastest. The strongest. The best.
The one and only. I AM STEVE.

You've got
weird feet.

WEIRD FEET STEVE!

Well, you smell.

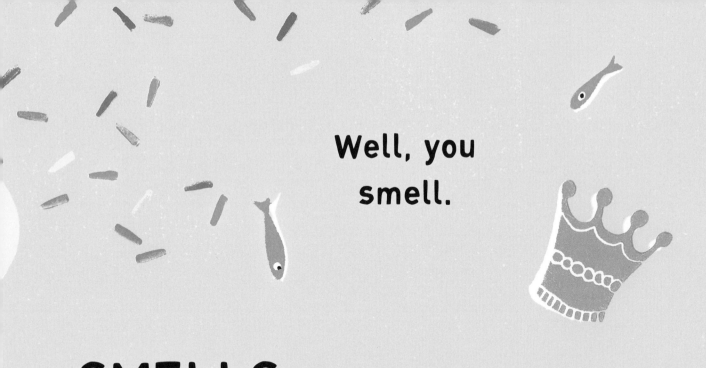

SMELLS
like
POO
STEVE.

I don't smell
like poo.

My feet
are fine.

Sorry, Steve.

Sorry, Steve.

Here
you go,
Steve.

Thanks,
Steve!

Hello!

I'm Steve.